# JoJo & Bow Bow

## THE POSH PUPPY PAGEANT

BY JoJo SIWA

**nickelodeon**

AMULET BOOKS
NEW YORK

Cataloging-in-Publication Data has been applied for and may be obtained from the Library of Congress.

ISBN 978-1-4197-3602-5
ebook ISBN 978-1-68335-545-8

Text copyright © 2019 JoJo Siwa
Cover and illustrations copyright © 2019 Abrams Books
Book design by Siobhán Gallagher

Printed and bound in the United States
10 9 8 7 6 5 4

Amulet Books are available at special discounts when purchased in quantity for premiums and promotions as well as fundraising or educational use. Special editions can also be created to specification. For details, contact specialsales@abramsbooks.com or the address below.

**ABRAMS** The Art of Books
195 Broadway, New York, NY 10007
abramsbooks.com

# CONTENTS

# CHAPTER 1

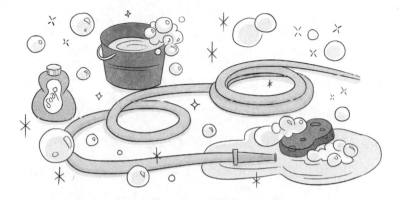

"**B**owBow, no!" JoJo Siwa didn't often say no to her cute, snuggly fur-ball friend, but BowBow Siwa didn't often jump paws-first into their neighbor's slimy green koi pond! "Get out of there now!" BowBow flattened her ears against her head and gave JoJo a look that said, *You can't possibly be mad at me!* Then she splashed her way back to the lawn, where JoJo stood waiting with her friend Jacob.

"Careful, JoJo," Jacob said. "Don't let Bow-Bow get too close! She's all muddy."

But it was too late. BowBow trotted right up to JoJo and shook out her fur, splashing green and brown muck everywhere.

"Oh, BowBow," JoJo said to the stinky teacup Yorkie, "you smell *terrible*."

"Yeah, that pond is more for looking at than for swimming," Jacob said. "It's my mom's thing. The whole garden is."

"Well, I hope your mom has a garden *hose*, 'cause BowBow's gonna need one! Luckily I wore old clothes today."

"Hose is on the patio," Jacob said.

JoJo scooped up BowBow in one hand and plugged her nose with the other, then headed for the patio while Jacob ran to collect a large plastic tub, a bottle of shampoo, and a handful of rags to use as towels.

"I've never given a dog a bath before," said Jacob, "but I grabbed Oscar's baby shampoo. My mom says it doesn't hurt if it gets into his eyes."

"That's perfect," JoJo said. "You're the best! Now, if only BowBow will stay still . . ."

But BowBow had other ideas. She splashed around the tub while JoJo squirted baby shampoo onto her fur and lathered her up, and soon Jacob and JoJo were both covered in suds.

"Phew," JoJo said a few minutes later. "I think we got all the pond muck out—we can set her down in the grass for a last rinse."

Jacob reached for the hose, and the two took turns squirting down BowBow, who yipped and ran in circles under the spray.

Then Jacob aimed the hose at JoJo!

"Jacob!" JoJo laughed, running away. Then she grabbed the hose from him and put her thumb in the middle of the spray so it would go all over the place. Soon she and Jacob were as soaked as her little pup!

By the time BowBow's bath was finished, all three were exhausted. JoJo and Jacob sprawled out on the grass, letting the bright California sun dry their T-shirts and gym shorts.

"Maybe we should toss BowBow back into the pond," Jacob suggested, flashing his blue braces as he smiled. "That was *fun*."

"Don't even joke about it!" JoJo giggled and turned over onto her stomach to check on BowBow. Her fur was already almost dry— she was so tiny that it didn't take much time.

"All that running around made me hungry," said Jacob, patting his stomach. "Want to grab a snack? I made double-chocolate caramel cookies last night."

"Of course you did," JoJo said with a grin. Jacob was always whipping up treats. "And yes, chocolate caramel cookies will totally hit the spot."

The two walked through the sliding glass door into Jacob's kitchen, BowBow at their heels. Jacob's mom was sitting at the counter with her laptop, and she gave them a big smile when they came in.

"Hey, kiddos," she said. "Looked like you were having fun out there!"

"BowBow jumped into the koi pond," JoJo told her. "But don't worry, she can swim."

"And don't worry, she doesn't like sushi," joked Jacob.

"Well, I'm glad of that," his mom said. "How about some peanut butter on a rice cake for BowBow and some cookies for you two? Unless you want sushi, that is," she said with a wink. "I think we have a fishing pole around here somewhere ..."

Jacob rolled his eyes at JoJo but smiled and

gave his mom a quick hug as he headed for the pantry and pulled out the ingredients for BowBow's snack.

"I'll leave you kids alone," Jacob's mom said, gathering her things. "I've got some work to do, and it looks like you've got your snacks under control. Nice seeing you, JoJo!"

As the two kids and BowBow were chomping away, the doorbell rang.

"That must be Miley," Jacob told JoJo. "I texted her while we were outside."

Miley, Jacob, and JoJo had been best friends for years. They'd met in the neighborhood when JoJo moved in, and they'd all quickly bonded. Then Kyra and Grace had moved in, and the terrific trio had become a fabulous fivesome.

Miley burst into the house without waiting for someone to let her in. "Hello?" She popped into the kitchen, her big smile warming JoJo, who skipped across the remaining distance to give her friend a hug. Jacob waved, his mouth full of cookie.

"Mmm, my favorite. How did you know?" Miley slid onto a barstool at the kitchen counter and grabbed a handful of cookies, then pulled out a glittery purple notebook. JoJo leaned over her shoulder as she opened it to a page that read, *Spring Fund-raiser.*

"What are you guys doing for your fund-raiser this year?" JoJo asked Jacob and Miley.

"That's actually why I asked Miley over," Jacob told JoJo. "We're allowed to team up with partners this year, and Miley and I decided to work together."

"Amazing," JoJo said. "You know I'm happy to help."

Every year, Jacob and Miley's school organized a spring fund-raiser. It wasn't mandatory, but the kids who wanted to participate could pitch an idea to the school principal for approval, and the proceeds of the individual fund-raisers went to the booster club. Lots of the older kids did car washes, and the younger kids usually did bake sales or lemonade stands with their parents' help. The events all took place on the same day at people's houses, in the school parking lot, or in the school gymnasium or cafeteria under the supervision of parents and teacher volunteers. JoJo always pitched in when her friends were involved, since she was homeschooled but liked to lend them a hand.

"Your bake sale last year was killer, Jacob," Miley told her friend. "Remember how fast you sold out of fudge pie?"

"Yeah! That was so fun! I'm just not sure I want to do it again this year. I kind of want to mix it up," Jacob said.

"Really?" Miley raised an eyebrow. "Seems like baking would be appropriate. And it's your favorite activity!"

"What do you think they're going to do with the money?" JoJo asked.

"Mrs. Shannon is head of extracurricular activities, and she said it depends on how much we raise. That's why I want to do something creative that will really make a profit."

"What are Grace and Kyra doing?" JoJo wanted to know.

"Well, you know how Grace's face painting was such a hit at the neighborhood block party?" JoJo nodded—Grace was a very talented artist! "She and Kyra decided to offer babysitting at the school gym for parents who want to explore the other fund-raisers at the school or in the community," Miley continued. "And Grace is going to make face painting one of the activities."

"That's so perfect," JoJo replied. "And Kyra is *great* with little kids."

"She babysat Oscar last week," Jacob piped up, spraying crumbs across the counter. "He loves her."

"Now, how can we come up with something creative and fun like that?" Miley pulled her eyebrows together, looking puzzled. "Oh!" she squealed in surprise as BowBow's moist nose touched her ankle under the barstool. "I didn't see you there, BowBow." She stooped down and scooped up the little dog, cuddling her close. "Mmm, BowBow, you smell good. And you're a little bit damp. Did you just have a shampoo?"

Jacob and JoJo exchanged a look, then burst out laughing.

"We gave her one in the backyard," JoJo said. "It was an emergency situation."

"Really? You did an awesome job," Miley said. "If only you could give her a haircut too."

"No way," Jacob said. "She'd probably come out looking like a mini Chewbacca!"

"It would be fun to do a spa day with her, though," JoJo mused aloud. "Once, I saw some nail polish and hair color for dogs at a pet store. I've been wanting to try them forever."

JoJo looked up to see Miley staring at her intently with a gleam in her eye. She knew that look! Miley's eyes sparkled like that when she had a big idea . . .

Then JoJo got it. "Miley, are you thinking what I'm thinking?" JoJo asked. Her best friend nodded and grinned.

"What?" Jacob looked back and forth between the two of them. "What are you guys thinking?"

"A dog wash!" JoJo cried just as Miley shouted, "A puppy spa!"

"Yes, that," they both said. "Jinx." Then they giggled, and Miley let loose her signature snort, making them giggle even harder.

"It's perfect, Jacob," JoJo said to her friend, when they had settled down. "Think how much fun we had today! All we have to do is offer to give baths to the neighborhood dogs! People can drop them off, and we'll wash them up."

"And maybe give them a little extra sparkle," Miley added.

"And then they'll pick them up at the end of the day. It won't even be work, because we'll have all the adorable pups to play with all day long! We can do it right here in your backyard—you already have some of the supplies. We can gather our allowance money for the rest, or ask our parents to pitch in. Maybe some local businesses will even donate."

"I know!" Miley looked up from her notebook, where she'd been scribbling notes. "When all the puppies are clean and sparkling, we can do a puppy pageant to show them off."

"And the pageant winner will get an amazing prize," JoJo finished. "It's perfect! Oh my gosh. It's going to be the best day ever."

Miley giggled and rolled her eyes at JoJo. "You're always saying that," she told her.

"Because it's true!" JoJo protested. "They're all the best day, until another, better day comes along. I can't help it that there are so many incredible days. Jacob—what do you think?"

"I don't know," Jacob said, looking worried. "I'd have to ask my mom. She may not want all those dogs running around."

"Well, then," JoJo said, "we have some convincing to do!" When JoJo and her friends had a great idea, they were unstoppable.

# CHAPTER 2

"Looks like you're doing some important work," JoJo's mom, Jessalyn, teased as JoJo bent over her phone, her thumbs moving furiously. Jess brought a bowl of strawberries and fresh whipped cream to the table, placing it next to JoJo's bowl of oatmeal. It was ten the next morning, and preparations for the fund-raiser were well under way. Miley had texted that she and Jacob had gotten the principal's stamp of approval and a hearty "Good luck!" in an email earlier that morning. "Is it your Instagram or YouTube?" Jess asked, digging into her own breakfast.

"Neither, actually," JoJo replied. "It's for the fund-raiser at Jacob's. I'm texting Grace about designing a flyer to promote our dog wash and pup pageant."

"Great idea," Jess responded. "I'm proud of you for helping your friends."

Just then, JoJo's phone pinged with an incoming text.

*<3 it!! Of course I'll do the flyer. Coming atcha soon,* said Grace.

"This is going to be amazing!" JoJo exclaimed. "It's all starting to come together."

"You and your friends make a great team," Jess replied. "What's on the schedule for today?"

"We're going to go to the pet shop

downtown to see if they'll donate any supplies," JoJo told her mom. "Jacob's mom offered to take us. I think she knows the owner. Then when Grace is done with the flyer, we'll make copies and post them around the neighborhood. We'll probably also make a few posters for Jacob's street and driveway, to point people in the right direction on Saturday."

"That's a lot for one day," Jess said. "Are you sure you can handle it all?"

"Well, today is already Wednesday, so we have to be on the ball! And it's the last few days of spring break before Grace, Miley, Kyra, and Jacob go back to school—we want to hang out as much as possible before then. Grace and Kyra don't need to do too much prep for their own project, since it's mainly babysitting. They're excited to help with Jacob and Miley's plan."

"Perfect," Jess said, taking one last bite of

her strawberry-topped oatmeal. "You know where to find me if you need anything."

"Love you, Mom," JoJo said. She gave her mom a quick hug, then bent to give BowBow a kiss on the top of her scruffy head before hurrying out the door.

No Bones About It was mostly empty when JoJo, Miley, and Jacob arrived. Kyra and Grace couldn't join them until later on—they were busily working on Grace's flyer as well as gathering supplies for fun activities they'd organized to keep toddlers entertained: crafts, finger paints, and games.

"You know," Jacob said, picking up a plush taco with a squeaker inside, "I asked around last night, and apparently the booster club might open a cooking lab with Mrs. Shannon's help if we earn enough money from the fund-raiser this year."

"No way!" said JoJo. "Like a *Top Chef* kind of thing?"

"Not *that* fancy," Jacob said.

"And not on TV!" said Miley.

"But, yeah! We'd have cooking workshops and sometimes even guest teachers, like the chef from Fortune's." Fortune's was a bakery in town. It was so popular that its signature dessert—the rocky road cannoli—sold out every day by noon.

"Whoa! Jacob, being a pastry chef is your dream," JoJo said. "How amazing to have a place to learn all about opening your own bakery and making your favorite treats."

Jacob nodded, looking shy. "I'm just really hoping it happens. It would be so cool to take classes with real chefs."

"We'll definitely do our part to help," JoJo assured him. "And come on. Who *wouldn't* want us to give their dog a bath?" JoJo put a dog-size cowboy hat on her head and struck a pose.

"Meanwhile," Miley piped up, "how many of these things do we have to buy to keep all the pups happy on the big day?" She tossed a fuzzy blue hippo at JoJo, who caught it, laughing.

"I think tennis balls will do the trick—and we have boatloads in our garage," JoJo said.

"Can I help you kids?" An employee approached them with an easy grin and a name tag that read Mandi.

"Hi, Mandi," said JoJo, sticking out her right hand. "I'm JoJo, and these are my friends, Miley and Jacob."

Mandi's eyes widened. "JoJo . . . Siwa?" she asked. "My niece is a *huge* fan of yours!"

"That's great to hear!" said JoJo. "Please tell her hello for me. Or, even better, if you have a phone, I can do it myself!"

A minute later, Mandi was back with her phone, and the two recorded a video for Mandi's niece, Lila—that way she'd have it forever. "Thanks, JoJo," she said when they were done. "You just won me the Aunt of the Year Award!"

JoJo grinned. "Always happy to help."

"Now, what can I do for you three?" Mandi asked.

"Well," Jacob chimed in, "we're organizing a fund-raiser for our middle school—we're going to hold a dog wash in my backyard."

"And a pup pageant afterward," Miley added. "We're looking for any donations that might help."

"How fun!" Mandi exclaimed. "I'll have to ask my boss. We're usually happy to do this sort of thing in exchange for a shout-out. We love the extra advertising! But just between us, business has been a little tight this year. I'll have to go check to make sure it's okay."

A minute later, Mandi was back with a whole shopping cart full of goodies. There were bottles of dog shampoo and conditioner, lavender-scented fur oil, and even nontoxic "paw-lish" for dogs' toenails!

Miley looked at it in wonder. "We can have all of this, for free?"

"Sure can," said Mandi. "We're happy to help. Turns out my manager's daughter is also a huge fan of yours, JoJo! Just be sure to put in a good word for us with your customers!"

"We will," sang JoJo, grabbing the bags of loot. They all thanked Mandi and waved goodbye, piling back into Jacob's mom's SUV.

"Wow," said Jacob's mom. "You guys got all of that with the ten dollars I donated to the cause?"

"Nope," Jacob told her, handing back her bill. "Turns out No Bones About It was willing

to donate to our cause . . . and they're huge fans of JoJo's too."

"Oh, pshhh," said JoJo, waving off the attention. "We'll have to ask Grace to print on the flyer that No Bones About It donated all the yummy-smelling supplies!"

Grace and Kyra were waiting on Jacob's front porch when they pulled into his driveway.

"Hey, guys!" Grace flipped her long red hair behind her shoulders and gave them a wave. Her friendly smile showed off the bright pink of her colorful braces.

"I bet she's already finished the flyer!" exclaimed Miley, scrambling out of the car just as soon as Jacob's mom cut the engine.

Sure enough, Grace drew a flyer from her backpack, and Kyra clapped excitedly. "She really outdid herself this time," said Kyra, and JoJo smiled at Kyra's praise. Kyra and Grace had had a rocky start when they first met, but now they were the best of friends.

The group huddled over the flyer, which was—as expected—absolutely amazing. Across the top it read, *Dog wash Saturday! We'll get your pups squeaky-clean! Immediately followed by a pup pageant. Winner gets a grand prize!* Underneath the text were pups of all sizes and shapes prancing across the page—

and, best of all, the illustrated dogs were sparkling with glitter!

"You guys know that glitter is my favorite thing!" JoJo exclaimed.

"I could have done with a little less *pink* glitter," Jacob chimed in. But he was smiling.

"Lucky for you, Jacob, glitter won't show up in the copies we make! The original is for you to keep," Kyra explained.

"You guys rock," Miley said. "One thing— would you mind putting a shout-out for No Bones About It at the bottom? They donated all our dog wash supplies."

"No prob," Grace agreed.

"This is bee-yoo-tiful," Miley added. "You two are incredible."

"I helped sprinkle the glitter," Kyra said proudly. "But Grace did all the drawing, of course. What's the grand prize, by the way?"

"Two tickets to be JoJo's guests at the

Nickelodeon Kids' Choice Awards," said Miley. "Donated by JoJo and approved by the school. But, shhh, don't tell anyone—it's a surprise."

"That's awesome," Kyra said. "I want to be your guest, JoJo! But I don't have a dog to enter in the puppy pageant."

"That's okay, Kyra. My mom already said all four of you can be my special guests this year."

Her friends cheered, and JoJo grinned. "You guys are the best, most supportive friends," she said. "There's no way I'd leave you behind!"

"No—you are," Jacob told her seriously. "What would we do without you? You've already helped us get all these amazing supplies. You're always supportive of us, JoJo."

"But I wouldn't be where I am without my friends," JoJo pointed out.

"Aww," Miley said. "Come on, guys—you

know I'm all about the lovefest, but we have to distribute the flyers before it gets dark! And we still have about a million copies to make!"

"Yes," called Jacob's mom from the kitchen. "Dinner's on in an hour, kids. We're having extra-cheesy lasagna. You're all invited!"

"And my famous peach shortcake for dessert," added Jacob.

"When you're the star of your own baking show, I want to be *your* guest, Jacob," said JoJo.

"Hear, hear!" chimed in Kyra, Miley, and Grace. Then they were off. They had work to do!

# CHAPTER 3

"**B**owBow, are you excited?" JoJo jumped out of bed and danced around her room with BowBow under one arm. Finally, the day of the fund-raiser had arrived. "Think of all the cute dog-friends you'll meet today!"

The plan was to meet at Jacob's at 10 a.m. to prep. People could drop off their dogs starting at noon and come back a few hours later for the pageant. It was foolproof! JoJo couldn't wait to hang out with a big bunch of doggies

all day long, but she worried that too few customers would come, and she knew how much Jacob and Miley wanted the fund-raiser to succeed.

Which is why she decided to post an extra-special photo on her Instagram.

"Sit, BowBow!" she said, and her pup obediently sat on the shaggy pink carpet.

"Hmm . . . I think we need a finishing touch." BowBow waited patiently while JoJo went to her closet and rifled through her bow collection. "Perfect!" she exclaimed, pulling out a teeny-tiny, glittery blue bow. She clipped it to BowBow's fur and took a step back, looking at her dog. "You're so cute, Bowbow!" In response, BowBow sat on her hind legs and lifted her front paws in the air, sittin' pretty. JoJo snapped a bunch of shots with her phone. BowBow was a pro!

Then JoJo uploaded the best photo to her

Instagram stories with the caption, *BowBow is sittin' pretty, and soon your dog will be too! Come to the dog wash and pup pageant! Pageant winner gets two tickets to the Nickelodeon Kids' Choice Awards!!!!* Then JoJo instructed people to DM her for the address and shared her story with followers she knew lived nearby—which was a lot! But she really, really wanted the fund-raiser to succeed, for Jacob's sake.

When JoJo arrived at Jacob's house an hour later with BowBow in tow, she gasped. "Uh-oh," she said. "This time I've really done it!" There was already a line of customers curving around the block! About two dozen owners and dogs were looking *very* disgruntled—and it wasn't even noon yet! JoJo headed for Jacob's backyard while sending an SOS text to Miley, Kyra, and Grace—they'd need major backup if they were going to pull off this dog wash.

When JoJo unlatched the gate to the back-yard, she found Jacob in a panic.

"JoJo, did you *see* how many people are out there? It's crazy! How will we wash all those dogs?!" Jacob's face was turning red, like it always did when he got upset. "My mom is going to kill me!"

JoJo's phone was pinging with texts from her friends. "Hang on," she said to Jacob. "I asked Kyra and Grace for help and texted Miley to see if she's almost here."

"Kyra and Grace have their own fund-raiser to run," Jacob said, moaning. "I don't understand—how did so many people find out about it? What will we do?"

"Well, for starters, we don't have to wait until noon," JoJo told him. "We can start now if your mom is okay with it. I think we're pretty well set up." She gestured at the buckets, dog brushes, and shampoos. "Secondly,

Miley just said she's two minutes away. And Kyra and Grace are sending over Grace's big sister to give us a hand. According to Grace, Megan *loves* dogs and is excited to help."

"Okay," Jacob said. "But we only have one hose!"

"We'll do an assembly line," JoJo assured him. "Someone will lather, someone will rinse, someone will dry, someone will brush. You'll see, it'll all work out."

Jacob nodded, seeming reassured. "Okay. I'll clear it with my mom." JoJo watched as Jacob jogged over to the screen door, then disappeared inside the house. While he was gone, JoJo began filling up the basin from the hose. It was a hot day, even for California, and the cold water felt refreshing against her fingertips. A couple of minutes later Jacob was back, and JoJo turned the nozzle to the off position, then turned to him for the verdict.

"Mom says it's okay—let's do it." He took a deep breath and walked out of the backyard through the gate and toward the driveway. "Let the dog wash begin!" JoJo heard him shout. And then there was a wild pitter-patter of paws on the driveway as dozens of dogs scampered for the backyard.

"Uh-oh, BowBow," JoJo whispered to her pup. "What have I gotten us into?"

JoJo was covered in suds and lathering up a cute, wrinkly pug puppy when Mandi and Miley walked into the yard.

"I would hug you, but I can't let go of this squirmy puppy!" JoJo called out in Miley's direction. "Plus I don't want to—she's so cute! Mandi, how did you know where to find us?"

"Miley told me," Mandi said, beaming. "It's my day off, and I wouldn't miss a chance to help. Plus, I brought Lila and Fig." A little girl stepped from behind Mandi, looking shy. She cradled a scruffy little mutt to her chest.

"Hi, Lila," said JoJo warmly. "Thanks for joining us. Does Fig need a bath?"

Lila nodded and smiled, stepping tentatively forward. "But we can wait until you're done with your other customers," she told JoJo, blushing. "For now, I'm here to help."

"We could use it! Fig can run around with the other pups while we're working," JoJo suggested. "The backyard is fenced in."

Just then, they heard a yell.

"Muddy dog alert!" shouted Jacob. "We forgot to fence off the koi pond!"

"Oh, no!" Mandi exclaimed. "I'll take care of that. Lila, you've helped me plenty at the shop—you know what to do." The smaller girl

34

nodded and got right to work, filling up a tub with soapy water and motioning for the next customer to step forward—unfortunately, with a Saint Bernard! A Saint Bernard with an even greater leash—it was adorned with sparkly rhinestones.

"You sure you can handle that one, Lila?" JoJo was worried. Lila was so small, and the dog was so big.

"I'm an old pro," Lila assured her with a grin. Then she got right to work, and soon the Saint Bernard was covered in mounds of thick white suds.

When JoJo handed off Cashew, the pug puppy, to Jacob to be toweled off, she took a minute to survey the operation. She waved at Megan, who must have shown up when JoJo was busy. Mandi appeared to be keeping things in order—handing supplies to Miley, Megan, Jacob, and Lila and lending an expert hand where needed. Jacob's mom had fenced off a portion of the backyard with baby gates from Oscar to form a mini dog run away from the commotion, and the clean pups were playing there. The line had shrunk to fewer than a half dozen people waiting to drop off their dogs. Everything seemed to be under control.

JoJo breathed a huge sigh of relief. For a minute, she'd thought her plan had backfired. But now she saw that it was the same in dog washing as it was in performing: If she put her head down and gave it her all, things tended to work out.

JoJo walked over to the gate to the backyard, BowBow at her heels, then opened it up and motioned for two more customers to come on in. "You can come back in three hours for the pup pageant," she instructed one woman with long blond hair, whose

fluffy white bichon was walking *her* into Jacob's backyard.

"Daisy likes hypoallergenic, vanilla-scented shampoo," the woman said, "and *hates* other dogs."

"No problem," Mandi said, stepping up behind JoJo. "We've got this under control." The woman sniffed and cast a doubtful look around the yard, but handed over Daisy's leash.

"I'll be back after my manicure," she informed them. "And Daisy would like one too."

"Thank goodness for you," JoJo told Mandi after waving goodbye to the blond lady. "New friends are the best! How did you get interested in working with animals, anyway?"

"In college I'm studying to be a veterinarian," Mandi replied. "And I've been working at the pet shop every summer and on school breaks for years. But that might be coming to an end. We haven't had a lot of customers since that big chain pet store opened over on Elm, and I'm worried our little shop might close." She gave JoJo a worried frown, then led Daisy over to the suds station.

"Not if I have anything to do with it." JoJo looked down at BowBow and winked at her pup, then knelt down and held up her right palm. BowBow gave her a high five with one little paw, then barked and began running around in circles. BowBow was as determined as JoJo was to make this day a success—for everyone.

# CHAPTER 4

"**H**i, Louis," JoJo heard Miley say as she let in a new customer. "What are you doing here?"

"Miley!" JoJo exclaimed from the suds station, where she'd taken over while Lila was in the bathroom. She shot Miley a stern look. Miley glanced back at JoJo and rolled her big dark eyes in the direction of the bespectacled boy who was waiting with what looked like a poodle–Chihuahua–basset hound mix. It was an adorable mash-up of curly and small, with giant floppy ears as big as its body and a long, old-man face.

"Come on in," Miley told the boy without enthusiasm. JoJo shot a smile his way and motioned him in, to make up for Miley's tone. JoJo was a firm believer in being kind no matter who the customer was.

"What's going on?" she whispered to Miley as Miley moved closer. "Be nice!"

"Well, *he* isn't nice," Miley whispered back with a shake of her curly brown hair. "He calls me 'Popsicle Stick' and 'Nerd Girl' at school just because I'm skinny and like to read!"

"That isn't nice," JoJo agreed. "But you're a Siwanator, Miley. Siwanatorz are kind, even to bullies. Being kind is practically the motto for our group! We band together against bullies—we don't stoop to their level."

Miley sighed. "Fine," she said, speaking

up now. "You can leave your dog with us, Louis. Feel free to come back at four for the pageant."

"I don't leave Winslow unattended," Louis told them, frowning over the collar of his crisp blue button-down. "I'll just sit over on that bench and watch."

"So you're not doing a fund-raiser of your own?" Miley wanted to know. "Are you just here because you're a fan of JoJo?"

"Don't be silly!" Louis colored. "I hardly even know who JoJo is. No offense," he said to JoJo, and she smiled and shrugged. "I don't believe in lots of screen time. But my little cousin is into dancing and loves your You-Tube videos, so that's how I've heard of you. As for my bake sale . . ." He looked down at the ground. "It's doing great. It's doing so great that it's practically running itself."

"You're welcome to hang out in the garden," JoJo told him, ignoring Miley's frown.

"Unless you want to lend a hand," Miley suggested.

"No thanks," Louis said. "I'd hate to get my nice clothes dirty." He handed Miley Winslow's leash and walked over to a bench on the opposite side of the lawn.

"And I'm the nerd?" Miley asked JoJo, who giggled.

"He just seems shy," JoJo said. "I bet he's nice once you get to know him."

"Maybe." Miley was doubtful. "His dog is super cute, anyway. I'll get Winslow started!"

JoJo was so busy that the minutes whizzed by. She nearly forgot all about Louis hanging out in the yard. She only hoped they'd finish up in time for the pup pageant. She'd brought over a box of costume supplies from her own years in dance recitals—there were sparkly scarves and tiaras and tutus for the dogs, from the times BowBow had been part of her act. It was going to be so cute!

There were only three dogs left to go when JoJo heard Megan let out a yell.

"Oh, no!" she shouted. "Daisy is *blue*!" JoJo whirled around to see Grace's big sister holding the formerly white bichon in the air. Sure enough, Daisy was a bright shade of turquoise. She looked like a giant, colorful marshmallow!

"How did that happen?" Jacob's face was reddening. "Mandi? Was there something in the soap?"

"Nothing that would turn her blue," Mandi said, looking stunned. "That's the hypoallergenic soap Daisy's owner requested. Ms. Rudolph will be so upset."

"Don't worry," JoJo said, patting Mandi's shoulder. "It isn't your fault. We used it on that little chow-chow mix over there, and he did just fine. Jacob, who was last with the soap?"

Jacob didn't have a chance to answer, because just then, Lila rushed over.

"You guys," she said, near tears, "one of the dogs is missing from the dog run!"

"What? How? Which one?" Miley had joined them, her hands on her hips.

"The Saint Bernard!" Lila gasped.

"How on earth did we lose a Saint Bernard?" Mandi looked confused. "Peppa was the biggest dog here!"

"And my mom's garden is half crushed," Jacob wailed, noticing a patch of trampled flowers near where they stood. "This is terrible."

"None of the owners will want to donate to our cause if there's a lost dog and a blue dog," Miley said. "What will we do? 'Best day ever,' huh, JoJo?"

"Everyone, just calm down," JoJo said. "We'll fix this. And yes, Miley. Sometimes even the best days experience curveballs. We need a minute to think. And we need everyone to pitch in. Maybe Louis can help." They all glanced toward the garden, and that was when they realized that Louis was no longer sitting on the bench.

"So much for watching Winslow," Miley muttered.

"Unless . . ." Jacob looked very, very upset, his face now a deep shade of purple. "You don't think . . ."

"Let's not jump to conclusions," JoJo said. "It was probably just an accident. Everyone, branch out. Peppa can't have gone far!"

A few minutes later, Megan came rushing over to where JoJo stood by the makeshift dog run.

"You guys," she said, "I hate to say this, but I found this bottle of blue dye next to the bench where Louis was sitting."

"And the side door to the house is open," said Jacob, huffing, as he joined them. "And there are muddy paw prints inside. Peppa must have run through the garden! My mom is going to be so mad."

"There are crumbs and rainbow-colored frosting *everywhere*," Mandi informed them. "Almost like Peppa got into a giant birthday cake before she broke free."

"A cake from a bake sale?" Miley asked. "*Louis's* bake sale?"

"Peppa and Louis are nowhere to be found," Jacob said, miserable. "The paw prints led to the front door."

"I think Louis is trying to sabotage our fund-raiser," Miley said.

"I don't think he's trying. I think he's already done it," Jacob replied.

"And if word gets out that one of the store's shampoos made Daisy blue, Ms. Rudolph won't stop until everyone in town knows," Mandi put in.

"Everyone. Take a deep breath," JoJo said. "We will find Peppa. We will get this under control."

But despite her confident words, JoJo wondered if their brilliant idea had turned into a paws-itive disaster.

# CHAPTER 5

"I don't understand," Jacob said. "Why would Louis do something like this?"

"Are you sure it was purposeful?" Jacob's mom asked. They were all standing in the kitchen while the kids explained the situation. "Don't jump to conclusions before you have all the information. Right now, let's just worry about finding that lost dog! Why don't you kids search the neighborhood with Megan? Mandi, Lila, and I will stay here to finish washing the remaining dogs, play with the others, and clean up this mess." She gestured at the trail of muddy paw prints and colorful crumbs that led from the back porch, through the kitchen, and straight to the front door. "If only I hadn't been upstairs when all of this happened!"

"I'm sorry about the mess," Jacob said.

"And your smashed flowers," Miley added.

"My smashed flowers? Oh, my . . ." Jacob's mom rubbed her forehead.

"Oops. Sorry, Jacob," whispered Miley.

But Jacob's mom only sighed, then laughed. "Don't worry about the flowers. I knew when you kids wanted to do a dog wash and pup pageant that there would probably be a few snafus. But I let it happen because I wanted you to learn how to take charge and handle responsibility. Running a business is hard— even for just a day! But you've done a great job so far, with the help of your friends. Asking for help is sometimes the best thing a person can do. Now, go find Peppa! You've still got an hour before the pageant begins."

"You're the best, Mom," Jacob said.

"Well, I want you to be a successful bakery owner one day," she told him, giving Jacob a kiss on the top of his head. "Better to learn these lessons now!"

"Moms *are* the best," JoJo agreed, thinking of how lucky she was to have her own mom in her corner. "Now, let's go find Peppa!"

Miley, JoJo, Megan, and Jacob followed the muddy footprints out the front door of Jacob's house and down the path to the sidewalk. There, the prints started getting fainter, but the group could see that Peppa had taken a right turn at the front gate. Luckily, even though the footsteps were fading, the crumb trail remained.

"This is so weird," Megan commented. "Why do you think there are so many crumbs? Are we sure they have anything to do with Peppa?"

"We don't have much else to go on," JoJo said. "Does anyone know which house is Louis's?"

Megan shook her head, and Miley frowned, looking discouraged.

"So I suggest we follow this trail. And we'd better hurry—looks like *someone* thinks our trail of clues is its afternoon snack." JoJo pointed at a bird that was pecking at the crumbs a half block ahead. Soon it was joined by another bird.

"Oh, no! Scram, birds!" Jacob quickened his pace, jogging up to the birds to shoo them away.

The crumbs with the rainbow frosting led all the way to the end of the block, where they stopped just in front of a large tan house with a broad front lawn.

"It's got to be here," JoJo told the others. "I'll go ring the bell. You guys stay on the lookout in case Louis tries to make a break for it!"

JoJo walked up the front path and rang the doorbell. She heard footsteps approaching, and for a minute she was hopeful. Then an older woman about the age of JoJo's grandmother opened the door.

"Hello," the woman said. "Can I help you, dear?"

"I'm looking for Louis," JoJo told her, peering around the woman and listening for the pitter-patter of doggie paws. There was only silence. JoJo felt her heart drop.

"There's no Louis here," the woman replied. "I'm sorry, honey. You must have the wrong house."

"Do you know where Louis lives?" JoJo asked.

"I'm afraid not," said the woman. "I'm new to the neighborhood. But it's lovely to meet you!"

"Nice meeting you too, ma'am," JoJo said. "Thanks anyway!"

The woman gave her a smile, and JoJo turned toward the hopeful faces of her friends, gathered on the sidewalk. *Now what?* she thought. She was beginning to worry.

"No luck," JoJo told the others as she crossed the yard to join them. "I just don't know what to do. Maybe we should turn back."

"We could ring all the doorbells in the neighborhood," suggested Jacob. "Someone's got to know where Louis lives."

"Maybe," Miley chimed in. "But that's *if* Louis really is the culprit! After all, he did leave Winslow behind. Maybe someone kidnapped Peppa *and* Louis!"

Jacob gasped. "Oh, no! I didn't even think about that! We've got to get my mom involved."

"I agree," JoJo said, uneasy. "I really thought this was a practical joke. Now I'm not so sure."

The group turned and began to walk back the way they'd come, in silence. They passed several houses and were nearly back to Jacob's when . . .

"Oh, fudge!" Jacob exclaimed, wrinkling his nose. "Ewww!" He held his foot in the air, showing the others the bottom of his sneaker.

"P.U., Jacob! Get that thing away from me!" shouted Miley. JoJo started to giggle. Jacob had stepped in a big pile of dog poo! Jacob rubbed his shoe on the grass, trying to scrape off the mess.

"Just what I needed," he grumbled.

"At least you spotted it before you walked inside your house," JoJo pointed out. "I think your mom's had just about enough disruption for one day! Hey, wait a minute . . ." She paused, looking at the mess Jacob's shoe left behind. "Wait just a minute!"

"JoJo, why do you sound excited?" Megan asked, wrinkling her nose.

"Doesn't that poo look a little *colorful* to you?" JoJo wanted to know.

"Yuck!" Miley shouted. "JoJo, cut it out!"

"No, look," JoJo insisted.

Jacob peered at the bottom of his shoe, then met JoJo's eyes. He grinned in excitement.

"You're right! It's got a bunch of weird colors in it, just like the frosting we spotted on the crumbs! It's rainbow-colored poo!"

"Peppa was here!" JoJo cheered. She didn't have to say another word. The whole group ran up to the house they were standing in front of.

JoJo rang the doorbell. There was no answer. She rang it again. Still nothing.

"There's a car in the driveway," Megan pointed out. "And lights on. I'll bet someone's home."

JoJo looked through the window next to the front door. There, hanging from the banister, was Peppa's rhinestone-studded leash!

"You guys, she's here! Peppa is inside," JoJo called out. She rang the doorbell again. "Louis, we know you're in there with Peppa!" she called. "We're not mad—just let us in!"

"Louis!" shouted Miley. "Louis, come out here right away and let us in."

"You guys . . ." Megan nudged JoJo and pointed to the gate that led to the backyard. It was hanging open. "I'm going to go take a look."

"You're going to snoop?" Miley looked horrified.

"I'll just take a quick peek. Maybe they're out back and can't hear the doorbell!"

JoJo said, "Good thinking, Megan. I'll come too." There was no time to lose—JoJo knew they had to bring Peppa back before her owner returned. JoJo and Megan poked their heads into the open gate and peered around the backyard. They didn't have to go inside to know it was definitely Louis's place.

# CHAPTER 6

"**O**h, no," JoJo said, taking in the scene. "I think I know what happened." She pointed at an abandoned stand with stacks of baked goods on top and a sign that read, *Louis's Bake Sale*. It had recently been dragged from out front, at least according to the telltale divots in the backyard. There were no customers in sight. JoJo had a sinking suspicion that she was partly to blame for that.

Then they heard the distinct sound of a dog barking. "Look!" shouted Megan. Peppa was in the back window, barking at JoJo and Megan! She appeared to be standing on a sofa, her front paws on the windowsill.

"Shhh," they heard. "Peppa, quiet!" Then Louis's face appeared beside Peppa's, looking out the window. His eyes widened when he saw them, and he ducked back out of sight.

"Louis! We see you!" JoJo wasted no time. She walked right over to the sliding back door and knocked hard until Peppa started barking again. "Louis! Let us in," JoJo said. "We're not mad." By then, Jacob and Miley had joined them in the backyard.

The door slid open just a crack. "You aren't?" Louis asked.

"We certainly *are*," said Jacob. "You ruined our fund-raiser and almost ruined the pet store's reputation!"

"And I'm also mad because you call me names at school!" Miley added.

"Shhh," JoJo said to Jacob and Miley. "I think I might know what happened here. Louis, can we come in and talk? We'll have to go get our parents if you don't hand Peppa over. It's probably better if you just talk to us."

A few seconds passed, and then the door slid the rest of the way open. Louis stood in front of them, looking miserable.

"I'm sorry," he said. "This whole thing was a dumb idea."

"We'll talk in a second," JoJo said. "First, I want to make sure Peppa is okay." She walked past Jacob into a large rec room. Peppa was most certainly okay! She was curled up on a sofa atop a mound of blankets, wagging her tail. There was a nature show on TV, and the soothing sound of tropical birds filled the

room. A big bowl of water sat on the floor next to the couch, and a plate covered in telltale rainbow crumbs was next to it. Peppa looked very happy!

"You've taken such good care of Peppa," Jacob said to Louis.

"Of course!" Louis said, sticking his hands into his pockets. "Winslow and I love other dogs! I dog sit all the time. Dogs are the best!"

"So why did you leave Winslow behind?" JoJo asked. "I thought you said you had to keep an eye on her."

"Oh, Winslow goes to doggie day care all the time," Louis said. "And she loves playing with other dogs. It's a treat for her. Plus, your mom was there. You mom is still there, right?"

"Yes. Watching all the dogs with Mandi and Mandi's niece, Lila," JoJo assured him. "So why did you say you had to stay and watch Winslow?"

"Just so you wouldn't think it was weird if I was around," Louis said. "Because I . . . well, I planned to borrow a dog."

"But *why?*" Jacob was furious. His hands were balled into fists, and his face had begun to flush. Louis was avoiding all their eyes. JoJo put a hand on Jacob's shoulder to calm him. She wanted to hear Louis out.

"I know it's awful," Louis began. "But I

was going to pick up Winslow and return the other dog after . . . well, later on today, after your fund-raiser had fizzled out. See, I thought I had a special idea for the fund-raiser this year. I love baking, so I always do a bake sale, and—"

"Your peanut-butter cookies are incredible," Miley broke in. "I love it when you bring them to school."

Louis gave her a small smile, and his cheeks turned pink. "Thanks, Miley. Baking—cooking in general—is my hobby," Louis said. "I really wanted to make a lot of money so we could have a real cooking lab at school! The only thing I love as much as baking is dogs," he added.

"Then why are you feeding poor Peppa a bunch of sugar?" Megan wanted to know.

Louis looked stunned. "I would never!" he

said. "That cake I gave Peppa is made from all-natural applesauce and peanut butter and carrots! The frosting is peanut butter and yogurt and organic food coloring. It's a totally dog-safe recipe. That's the whole thing," he went on. "I thought I'd combine my love for baking and my love for dogs and have a bake sale with treats for humans *and* dogs! There are so many dogs in this neighborhood. It was going to be perfect . . ." He looked miserable.

"Until I posted my Instagram story," JoJo finished. She felt bad. She had only wanted to help Jacob and Miley.

"What Instagram story?" Jacob asked just as Miley nodded in understanding.

"I wanted to get people to come to our dog wash and puppy pageant," JoJo explained. "I knew how much the fund-raiser meant to you."

"I love baking too," Jacob explained to Louis. "It's my favorite thing. I want to open my own bakery one day."

"Me too!" Louis's face glowed with excitement.

JoJo smiled. She knew a budding friendship when she saw one!

"But all the people with dogs came to our dog wash instead of your bake sale," JoJo finished for Louis.

He nodded, looking glum. "I spent weeks baking with my mom and dad," he said. "We made all kinds of special dog treats. And then there was no one to enjoy them."

"No one except Peppa, that is," Jacob joked. "Peppa is a very happy dog right now—your treats must be good!" They all laughed.

"But, Louis, we're all trying to raise money for the same cause," JoJo pointed out. "Why did you want our fund-raiser to flop? People could have gone to both our fund-raisers."

"I didn't want it to *flop*," Louis protested. "Well, not exactly, anyway. I was just afraid none of the people with dogs would come to mine, and I'd put in so much hard work. I guess I was jealous. You're right—now that I think about it, it didn't make much sense. I turned it into a competition when it didn't have to be."

"I wish you'd just come to us, so we could have talked about it and worked together," JoJo went on. Then her face paled. "Louis! Did you put dye in the shampoo also?" JoJo put her hands on her hips, facing Louis with a frown. In her opinion, that was going way too far.

"I did," Louis said. "But it was only organic dye for baking—it's edible! It won't hurt the dogs."

"Still," JoJo said, "it makes Mandi and the pet shop look bad. After all, they donated the supplies. And it's advertised all over our flyers. Now that Daisy looks like a blueberry, it might hurt the business."

"I didn't think of that," Louis admitted. "I'm so sorry. I'll make sure to apologize."

JoJo nodded. But she wasn't quite finished. "One last thing," she said. "Why did the crumbs trail end down the road rather than here at your place?"

"Oh, I just did that to throw you guys off track, in case you came looking. How did you find us, anyway?"

Jacob gestured to his shoes, which he'd placed right outside the door. "We had a smelly, rainbow run-in," Jacob told Louis.

"Gross!" But both boys were grinning.

"You know, Louis," Miley broke in, "people can still buy your treats."

JoJo beamed at her friend. She loved when Miley had a great idea! And she loved it all the more when they had great ideas at the same time. "That's exactly right," JoJo said. "It doesn't need to be a competition. Listen, Louis, all the dog owners are coming back to Jacob's house very soon to pick up their pets and watch the pageant. What if you sell your treats to the audience at Jacob's house?"

"Kind of like a concessions stand?" Louis said, looking thoughtful. "I love that idea!"

"Jacob, would it be okay with your mom?" Megan asked. "I think we have enough free hands to carry those treats back."

Jacob laughed. "I think my mom's seen it all by now," he said. "She won't mind."

"Then it's settled!" JoJo clapped her hands, and Miley gave Louis a hug.

He looked startled, and his blush deepened. "I'm sorry for calling you names, Miley," Louis told her. "It's just . . . I've always thought you were really nice. I wanted to be your friend, but I was never sure how to talk to you." He mumbled the last part, looking nervous.

"It's okay," Miley told him. "I *am* a nerd!"

"That's what I like about you!" Louis said, then looked embarrassed.

Miley laughed. "Let's get Peppa ready quick and gather up all your treats," she said.

"They're already in containers, because I started to put them away, thinking no one was going to eat them," Louis said. "I'll go get them now! And let me just call my mom and dad to let them know where I'll be." He turned toward the hall to the kitchen, then paused. "You guys?" he said, looking back. "Thank you for being so great about all of this. And I'm really, really sorry for what I did. It was wrong."

"It's okay," Jacob said. "But next time, just

talk to us if something comes up, and we'll figure it out." Jacob paused at the threshold to the kitchen. JoJo laughed as she saw him sniff the air. "Is that cinnamon I smell?" he asked. "And apples?"

"Yep. Apple tarts," Louis told him, getting excited. "Mini ones."

"They smell amazing," Jacob told his new friend. "You'll have to give me your recipe!"

Miley, Megan, and JoJo exchanged smiles as the two boys went into the kitchen to gather up the fresh pastries. It looked like a match made in culinary heaven!

"I'll go grab Peppa's leash," Megan said, skipping off in the direction of the front door. "It was the rhinestone one, right? No time to lose!"

Soon the group was gathered in the back of Louis's house, loaded up with Tupperware containers full of treats—for both dogs and people—and accompanied by one very excited pooch. "Off we go," said JoJo, leading the group back toward Jacob's. Everything had worked out—but it had been a close call. And the fun was just beginning!

# CHAPTER 7

All the pups were clean and dry when the group returned with Peppa. There were only twenty minutes to spare before the designated owner arrival time of 4 p.m. And they still had to do paw-dicures! Winslow greeted Louis with an enthusiastic, slobbery kiss.

"But Daisy is still blue," Jacob noted, looking upset.

"We washed her again," Mandi told him. "And the dye has faded a lot—see?" Jacob nodded, but JoJo could see that her friend was still worried. "It'll come out after a few more washes," Mandi said. "Meanwhile, I'm going to offer Ms. Rudolph a free grooming session at No Bones About It. She might be angry, but that should soften the blow."

"Thanks, Mandi," Jacob said.

JoJo looked down at Lila, who was staring up at her adoringly. JoJo loved kids, and she'd hardly had time to hang out with Mandi's niece. "Did you have fun playing with the dogs while we were gone?" she asked the smaller girl.

"Yes!" Lila grinned up at JoJo. "And Fig and BowBow are best friends. See?" She pointed at the two small dogs. Sure enough, they were playing with a ball in a corner of the make-shift dog run.

"She's having the time of her life," Mandi assured JoJo.

"Great!" JoJo said. "Why don't you help me set out dog costumes for the pageant, Lila? And we still have to do the paw-dicures for everyone who opted in." Lila nodded, smiling brightly, and followed JoJo over to the box of costumes. As they dug through the piles of glittery material, pulling out options that could work for each of the dogs, some of the owners began to trickle in.

"Cashew! You smell so fresh!" squealed one woman, who bent over the enclosure to the dog run and scooped up her pet. JoJo turned and smiled, watching the woman bury her face in the pup's fur. "Cashew definitely wants to be in the pageant," the woman informed Jacob, who was taking her donation. "My daughter, Carly, would love to be JoJo's special guest at the Kids' Choice Awards!"

"Sure thing," Jacob said brightly. "JoJo and our friend Lila are laying out all the costume options now. Feel free to go pick out a glittery sash for Cashew."

It went on like this for a while. People were ooohing and aahing over their pets, bringing them over to the paw-dicure station for Lila, Miley, and JoJo to touch up their nails, and swinging by the snack table, which Jacob, Louis, and Jacob's mom had laid out with all of Louis's delicious treats. It was like one big party! And best of all, JoJo's phone pinged with a message from Grace—she and Kyra were done babysitting and were heading over to help judge the pageant!

Everything was falling into place, and JoJo was having a blast with her friends. She and Grace and Kyra and Miley were clearing an area of the lawn for the pageant and bringing the guests cups full of lemonade that Jacob's mom had made. BowBow and Fig

and the rest of the dogs were scampering all over the yard in their costumes—everywhere *except* the koi pond, which was now off-limits to all the dogs: The friends had learned their lesson! JoJo sampled Louis's blondies as well as his chocolate cupcakes, and she had to say, Jacob had met his baking match! And Bow-Bow sampled Louis's rainbow dog cake. Louis and Jacob were getting along great, sharing recipes and trading tips. Best of all, the donations were rolling in. Jacob had had to empty the fund-raiser jar at least twice already.

JoJo was just helping a Chihuahua into a pizza costume when she heard a shriek from the back gate.

"Daisy!" the shrill voice called. "Daisy! It can't be you!"

The lawn fell silent, aside from the slobbery sounds of a terrier mix lapping up some water from its bowl. JoJo stood and watched

Mandi hand over little Daisy, now a pastel shade of blue. She held her breath. Louis and Jacob approached Ms. Rudolph, their eyes downcast. But before either boy could open his mouth to explain, Peppa's owner stepped in.

"My, what a gorgeous shade of blue," she remarked, patting Daisy on the head. "If my Peppa weren't dark brown, I'd certainly have requested this treatment! You're a lucky dog, Daisy."

Ms. Rudolph blinked and hugged Daisy closer. "Well . . ." she began, but then another guest cut in.

"I had no idea custom dyes were available!" said the owner of a sweet little Maltese. "I'd love to request one for next time. Who provided the colors?" The man picked up a flyer from the nearby snack table. "No Bones About It, eh? Well, I'll definitely be coming in for a grooming session for my Hamloaf."

"And we'd like to offer you a free grooming session, Ms. Rudolph, since Daisy was our very first model for the new dyes," said Mandi. "Bring her back anytime, on the house."

"Well," JoJo could hear Ms. Rudolph say over the buzzing of the crowd that had gathered around her and Daisy, "I suppose the blue does go nicely with Daisy's eyes."

JoJo and Miley looked at one another and exchanged relieved smiles.

"Phew," said JoJo. "I was afraid we were in for it!"

"Take a look," Miley said. "Mandi's giving out her business card!"

It was true: Mandi had run out of cards by then and was jotting down the pet shop's number on pieces of paper, which she handed out to everyone who asked. JoJo smiled; it looked like No Bones About It would have some steady business for a while.

"You guys sure know how to throw a party," said Kyra, heading over to JoJo with Grace in tow. Both girls were licking frosting off their fingers.

"And we needed that sugar after a full day of babysitting!" Grace exclaimed. "Great work, everyone."

"It's almost like we planned it," said JoJo, and she and Miley dissolved into giggles. Then she motioned to the others and pointed out a shady spot just in front of the area they'd cleared for the pageant. "You two sit there—you'll need a good view to judge the show."

"What about you, JoJo?" asked Grace.

"I'm handling the music!"

Jacob lined up all the pageant beauties while JoJo hooked up her microphone. The guests filed in to watch, and Louis settled himself on the opposite side of the stage from Jacob, with a big Tupperware container of dog treats in hand.

"Before we begin," JoJo announced, "we thought we'd get the party started with a song!" Everyone cheered—most of them were already fans of JoJo's music. "Kids are welcome to come dance with me up here," JoJo said, motioning for Lila, who was sitting cross-legged on the lawn, to join her. Lila hopped up and stood beside JoJo, and a few other kids who'd come with their parents joined them as well. Then JoJo queued up the music to "High Top Shoes." Everyone who knew the words started singing along, and soon it was a full-on dance party! JoJo always had a blast performing for friends and family but especially when kids who loved her music could sing and dance alongside her.

When the song wrapped up, everyone cheered, and JoJo handed off the mic to Jacob.

"Welcome to the first-ever Posh Puppy Pageant!" Jacob said into the mic, and everyone cheered again. "Our judges are Miley, Kyra, and Grace. We hope you all have fun watching these posh pups strut their stuff! First up, let's hear it for Cashew!"

The little pug's owner led her across the stage, where she accepted a treat from Louis. "Cashew is wearing a stunning glittery pink sash and sparkly blue nails," Jacob narrated, "but above all, she is an adorable fluff-ball with a dazzling smile!" The crowd roared.

Next came the pastel blue Daisy. Then an English cocker spaniel named Mochi, wearing tiny, rainbow-hued tutus on each paw. Then Fig and Hamloaf and Peppa and Winslow, as well as three other sweet mutts, a doxie, and a pair of min pins wearing T-shirts and tiaras. When it was all over, Grace, Kyra, and Miley put their heads together to confer. A minute later, they motioned JoJo over.

"We can't decide," Kyra said. "All the dogs are just so cute! And they all did a great job."

"I agree," JoJo said. "I wish we had a prize for everyone." Then she felt a tug on her shirt. Lila had crept up next to the older girls while they were talking.

"What about those tennis balls you brought from your garage?" she asked JoJo. "We never even needed to get them out for the pups to play with."

"Great idea, Lila! Tennis balls are perfect— and maybe goodie bags of leftover home-made dog treats, if there are any."

"We've got at least a few dozen," Megan said, joining them. "Louis really outdid himself! We already sold maybe two hundred of his pastries and dog treats. People bought entire bags of them! Apparently they freeze well."

"Two hundred?" JoJo said in disbelief. "That's incredible! We only had about twenty dogs here today."

"Yep." Grace smiled up at her sister. "It seems like all of our fund-raisers were a huge hit."

"I'll stall everyone with another song while you guys prep the goodie bags and write down all the names for a random drawing," said JoJo. "That seems like the fairest way to award the grand prize."

The others nodded and got to work. Then JoJo took the stage and began singing her classic hit, "Boomerang." The crowd went wild.

"We've come to a tough decision, folks," Jacob said into the microphone a few minutes later. "All of your dogs were just too darned adorable to decide on a winner, so we opted for a random drawing instead. All of your pooches' names are in this basket." Jacob gestured to the wicker plant-holder Kyra and Grace had brought him. "I'm going to shake it up, then choose a random name." Jacob paused, shook the basket a few times, then moved his hand around, pretending to draw out first one folded slip of paper, then another, teasing the crowd. Finally he pulled one slip of paper all the way out, unfolded it, and looked out at the audience.

"And the winner is . . ."

He cleared his throat then peered at the paper and squinted, as though having trouble making out the name. JoJo giggled to herself. She loved Jacob's hijinks.

"The winner is Fig!" he cried out. The whole lawn erupted into applause, and JoJo couldn't help but feel thrilled for her new friends. "Fig, Lila, and Mandi, please join me at the mic. You too, JoJo!" Jacob instructed.

JoJo rushed over to Jacob. She gave Lila and Mandi giant hugs, then accepted the mic.

"I'm so happy to present two tickets to the Nickelodeon Kids' Choice Awards to Lila, to use for herself and a parent. Or another relative," she added, winking at Mandi. "Without Mandi's and Lila's help today, we never could have pulled off the dog wash and pup pageant! Did everyone have fun today?" Everyone cheered in response. "Would everyone like to hear another song?" The crowd went wild. "Okay, then!" said JoJo. "But I want to see you guys dance it out!"

She launched into "Hold the Drama," grabbing Lila's hand and dancing with her around the lawn. Soon everyone—including the dogs—was bouncing around the yard to the beat of JoJo's music. No one could deny that the dog-wash-turned-puppy-pageant-turned-bake-sale-turned-dance-party was a huge success—maybe even the most fun fund-raiser ever!

# CHAPTER 8

"**N**ow for the good part," Jacob's mom said, handing each of the kids a garbage bag.

Jacob groaned. "Ugh. Do we have to?" he asked, plopping down in the grass. "I'm tired. And my stomach hurts!" By then, the crowd had tapered off, and the group of friends had even said goodbye to Mandi, Lila, Megan, Grace, and Kyra. Only Jacob, Louis, Miley, and JoJo remained. Jacob had invited them all to stick around for pizza, and, in turn, they'd offered to help clean up.

"Too many sweets?" his mom asked, giving him a stern look.

"It's the first time I've overdosed on cookies that I didn't bake myself!" Jacob said. "I'm pretty picky," he said, turning to Louis. "I usually only trust my own baking."

"It's true," JoJo said, laughing. "Louis, you should feel flattered!"

"All I feel right now is grateful to you guys for including me, after what I did," Louis said, sitting on the grass next to Jacob and pulling Winslow into his lap.

"That's what Siwanatorz are for," replied JoJo. "And it's why we started the group to begin with. Usually if there's a problem, it just takes trying to understand one another in order to work it out."

"Well I, for one, am glad we did," Miley added. "This was such a fun day! How much money do you think we brought in?"

"I'm not sure," Jacob said. "I gave it all to my mom to keep safe. I really, really hope it's enough for a cooking lab."

"A special oven has your names written all over it," JoJo assured Jacob and Louis. "How cool, though? I can't believe I know two great chefs!"

"I guess we'll find out for sure at school next week," Louis said, looking worried.

"Cleanup time!" shouted Jacob's mom through the screen door. "Enough chitchat. Pizza will be here in fifteen minutes."

JoJo shooed Winslow and BowBow inside with the permission of Jacob's mom, so the two dogs wouldn't get in the way of cleanup. Then the kids put all the plastic lemonade cups in a recycling bag and gathered the pet-wash supplies they could still use. Then they folded up the card table that had held Louis's treats, swept bits of cookies and cakes from the patio, folded all the pageant costumes neatly back into their box, and brought the baby gates inside.

Once inside, JoJo stretched, worn out from the day's activities.

"Everything looks great," Jacob's mom told them. "You kids must be starving. At least, those of you who didn't eat a dozen cookies!" She gave Jacob a look and shook her head but smiled.

JoJo dug into a giant slice of pepperoni pizza. They were seated on the floor of Jacob's TV room, watching a cooking show the boys had chosen. BowBow was curled up in JoJo's lap. It was nearly 7 p.m. by then, and JoJo was pooped. She giggled at the thought.

"Jacob, what did you do with your smelly sneakers?" she asked. "I still can't believe that poop was rainbow-colored!"

"I hosed them off when we got back, then put them in the wash," Jacob told her. "I wonder if BowBow will have rainbow poop after all those treats she ate."

"Ruh-roh," said JoJo to her sleeping pup, whose belly was looking awfully large. "I'll have to keep you posted."

"You guys," said Miley, "I'm really going to miss nights like these when we go back to school on Monday. Spring break has been a blast."

"It really has," JoJo agreed. "But time will fly. I'll be traveling during the week, and you guys will be in school and doing sports, and we'll still have our weekends. And the Kids' Choice Awards show is coming up!"

"I just really, really love our friendship," Miley said.

"Awww," said JoJo, leaning over to give her friend a hug.

"You guys are such saps," Jacob called out from where he sat in front of the TV.

"Don't think you're getting out of this," JoJo said, motioning him and Louis over. "Group hug!"

Jacob rolled his eyes, but Louis smiled, and both boys scooted closer to the girls and wrapped their arms around their shoulders. "I don't have a ton of friends," Louis told them, looking suddenly shy. "And I sure am glad today happened. I'm even glad I was kind of a jerk about things. Because I got to meet all of you!"

JoJo laughed. "Well, it worked out this time, but try not to be a jerk too often! You're officially a Siwanator now, and Siwana-torz believe in kindness." Then she yawned again—a big yawn.

"I've got to call it a night, guys. But this has been one of my favorite days ever," she told them. "All because of you."

JoJo thanked Jacob's mom for the pizza and walked BowBow home, savoring the cool spring air and the afterglow of a day well spent. JoJo unhooked BowBow's leash at their front yard, letting the pup run around a bit while JoJo checked the mail. She grabbed a stack of letters, including some fan mail for her and BowBow—*yay!*—they loved getting fan mail.

"Come on, BowBow," she called to the pup a minute later, as she headed toward the house. BowBow barked twice and ran ahead of JoJo, turning circles on the grass. They were nearly to the front door when she felt something squish beneath her high-tops. She froze.

"BowBow . . ." she said, looking down at the pup. Sure enough, BowBow was looking up at her with a guilty expression. JoJo held up her foot and shone her phone's flashlight at the sole of her sneaker.

"Yep. Rainbow all the way. Well, glad you got it out of you, at least!" JoJo slipped off her shoes and left them outside, giggling a little as she went into her house, hugged her mom, and started getting ready for bed.

# CHAPTER 9

"**M**om! BowBow's almost out of food," JoJo shouted up the stairs. It was a week and a half later, and JoJo had just finished her rehearsal for a concert she was performing at the end of the month.

"Okay," Jess called down. "We'll head over to the shopping center and pick some up. Maybe a little ice cream, while we're at it."

Although ice cream was a tempting offer, JoJo had another plan in mind. "Actually," she said as her mom came downstairs and joined her in the kitchen, "why don't we go to No Bones About It? I wouldn't mind saying hi to Mandi and seeing how business is going over there after the fund-raiser."

"Sounds good to me!" Jess said. "I love that you're supporting your new friend."

They piled into the car and made their way to the pet shop. JoJo made a short Instagram story as she went, keeping her fans posted on everything she'd been up to that day. Ten minutes later, they pulled into the parking lot in front of No Bones About It.

"Mom," JoJo said, carefully unbuckling her seat belt, "why are the windows dark? And why are there no cars in the lot? It's a Wednesday at three in the afternoon! Where are all the customers?"

"JoJo," Jess said, placing a hand on JoJo's arm, "please don't take it to heart if they closed. You did your very best to drum up business for the store."

"I'm going to go check it out." Before her mom could do anything to stop her, JoJo hopped out of the car and walked over to the shop. Sure enough, there was a closed sign in the window. JoJo was about to turn back, when she saw movement behind the glass. She knocked on the door. "Hello?" she shouted. She was going to get to the bottom of this, one way or another! JoJo knocked again, harder, until she finally heard the latch click. The door opened to reveal a smiling Mandi behind it.

"Mandi!" JoJo exclaimed. "What happened? Did the store close? Are you okay? What's going to happen?"

Mandi laughed. "JoJo, calm down!" she said. "Nothing bad happened. Quite the opposite, actually! We shut down the store for a week so we could expand. I was just working in the back—we're turning our old storeroom into an additional space for grooming. Business has boomed since the fund-raiser. Everything is going great."

"That's amazing!" JoJo threw her arms around Mandi and gave her a huge hug. "I'm so happy to hear that!"

"It's great news," Mandi agreed. "But wait—are you here just to say hi, or were you trying to buy something?"

"BowBow's out of kibble," JoJo said, "but don't even worry about it. We can go somewhere else."

"Don't you be silly," Mandi protested. "What kind does BowBow like?" JoJo told her, and Mandi ran to the back of the store, emerging with a jumbo bag. "On the house," she said, handing it to JoJo. "I can't ever repay you for everything you did for us."

"What are friends for?" JoJo asked, waving goodbye. "See you and Lila Saturday for the awards!" Lila had opted to bring Mandi rather than her mom or dad, since Mandi was more like a big sister than an aunt to her. JoJo was glad.

"We can't wait," Mandi called.

Back in the car, Jess smiled at JoJo. "Doesn't it feel good to help people?" she asked.

"Yeah! And to make new friends," JoJo agreed. "I'm so excited to take Mandi and Lila to the Kids' Choice Awards!"

"I'm thinking we'll have a little pre-party at our house beforehand for all your friends who are coming with you," Jess said. "We'll order pizza, get dressed up, hang out . . ."

JoJo and her mom discussed the awards the whole way home. It was going to be a blast. Every occasion with her friends was a great time, but the Kids' Choice Awards were extra-special fun, and they were only a few days away. JoJo even had the perfect outfit picked out for it. It was orange and green, custom-made, and sparkly all over, with a bow to match. And BowBow had a matching dog jacket. JoJo could hardly wait!

A few mornings later, the Siwa kitchen was stocked with boxes of doughnuts, cupcakes, and sparkling juice. It was eleven o'clock, and JoJo was still yawning the sleep away—she was *not* a morning person. But her friend Dee, who always did her hair and makeup for performances, was there. JoJo had just settled into the chair in her bathroom, getting ready for Dee to work her magic, when the doorbell rang.

"Hang on, Dee!" JoJo leapt out of the chair and rushed downstairs to see which of her friends it was.

"Surprise!"

JoJo yelped and jumped back—it was all of them! Even some of her friends from the town where she grew up in Nebraska had flown in to surprise her. Miley, Grace, and Kyra were holding balloons. And Louis and Jacob were holding a giant box between the two of them. JoJo could see some of her YouTube friends standing behind them too. And there were Mandi and Lila, her guests of honor.

"Oh my gosh, you guys!" JoJo was so excited, she nearly cried. "I didn't know you were all coming today!"

"We thought we'd throw together a real party," her mom said, coming up behind her. "I knew you'd want all your favorite people together on your special day! So I flew in a few of your friends from Omaha."

JoJo threw her arms around her mom.

"You thought right," she said, grinning from ear to ear. "I could not be happier. This is the best surprise."

"Maybe not the *best*," Jacob said, coming inside the house with the giant box. "Because what Louis and I have in here is the *best* surprise!"

"What is it?" JoJo peered at the box, which was so big, Jacob could hardly see over the top of it.

"Open it and see," Louis said.

JoJo opened the box—and gasped. Because inside it was the biggest, most colorful, most beautiful cake she'd ever seen in her entire life. It was orange and green and three tiers high, with edible sparkles and a giant edible Nickelodeon blimp on top.

"We made it together . . ." Louis began.

". . . with the help of a pastry chef from Fortune's . . ." said Jacob.

". . . who's going to be teaching workshops at our school's brand-new cooking lab!" finished Louis. "And that blimp is filled with chocolate custard. It's really an éclair masquerading as a blimp."

JoJo jumped up and down, squealing with excitement. "That is amazing!" she said. "And that sounds delicious. But when did you find out you'd met your fund-raising goal?"

"Last week," Jacob admitted. "Just about a week after we held the fund-raisers."

"But none of us wanted to spoil the surprise," said Miley. She helped Jess and JoJo take the cake from Jacob and set it gently on the kitchen counter.

"You guys are the best friends ever," JoJo said. "And this is shaping up to be the best *day* ever. I love you guys!"

"We love you, too, JoJo," Miley told her, giving her a huge hug.

"Do you kids want some pizza before we start getting ready for the awards?" asked Jess. "It's nearly noon now—your dad and Jayden should be back any minute from the pizza shop."

"No way," said JoJo. "We're starting with cake!"

A few hours later, stuffed to the brim with cake and pizza, JoJo, her family, and her special guests—Kyra, Grace, Jacob, Miley, Mandi, and Lila—were ready to go. The rest of the group planned to hold down the fort until JoJo returned for a post-party sleepover! JoJo was nervous, but in a good way. After all, the Kids' Choice Awards were her favorite day of the year. Next to Christmas. And her birthday. And BowBow's birthday . . . well, she had a lot of favorite days. But there was nothing she loved better than performing in front of her fans with all of the people she loved there to support her. And if she won an award—that was just the cherry on top! JoJo skipped over to the back door and hit the button for the garage. They needed to get going if they were going to be on time.

"JoJo, what are you doing?" her mom asked. "The car's out front."

"No, it's not," JoJo said, looking into the garage, where her family's car was parked.

"Not that car," JoJo's dad said. "The other car. The one we got for your big day! Go see."

"What did you do?" JoJo asked. She ran to the front door, her friends trailing behind. Her family was the best at planning surprises, and this time was no exception. There was a bright orange limousine idling in the driveway out front! JoJo couldn't help herself. She screamed.

"Oh my gosh, oh my gosh!" BowBow barked and hopped around at her feet. "You guys! This limo is the coolest! I can't believe you found one in orange—it's perfect for Nickelodeon."

"We thought you'd like that," JoJo's brother, Jayden, said. "Now come on—there are more surprises waiting inside!"

"I wish you could come, BowBow," JoJo told her dog, cuddling her close. "But this time you have to stay back. Don't worry—when I get home, I'll tell you all about it!" She offered BowBow a treat from the jar they kept in the front hall, then grabbed her phone and headed straight for the coolest, fanciest ride she'd ever seen.

The group heading to the awards piled into the limo. JoJo giggled at Lila, whose eyes were wide. Sure enough, the limo was decked out with streamers in slime-green and

109

Nickelodeon's signature orange. "Hold the Drama" was blaring through the speakers. The interior lights were flashing as though they were in a dance club, not a car. There was a mini fridge stocked with all kinds of soda and sparkling water, and on top of it was a tray piled high with all of JoJo's favorite candies.

"You guys!" JoJo said. "Did the limo come like this?"

"Of course not," Miley said. "I got here early and helped your dad and Jayden decorate, while your mom set up inside the house. It was a team effort."

JoJo hugged her friend.

"Turn it up!" Miley shouted toward the front. "Please, I mean."

"You got it," said the driver. And they all sang along to "Hold the Drama." Even Mandi joined in.

"Mandi, I didn't know you were a fan," Jacob told their new friend.

"Lila got me into JoJo's music," Mandi said. "I even know some of the choreography!" She acted out some of the moves, as best she could with her seat belt buckled. They all laughed and danced along, filled with the buzz of excitement.

Before they knew it, the group had arrived at the Kids' Choice Awards.

"Aw, man," Jacob said, disappointed. "I could have stayed in that limo forever."

"The fun is only just starting," JoJo told her friends. She knew the drill—she'd been to the awards before. "First, we'll walk the red—err, *orange*—carpet, and then you'll meet all my other friends, before we have to be seated for the awards."

Time flew by from there. JoJo loved seeing her friends go wild over all the stars of their favorite Nickelodeon shows. And JoJo introduced them to everyone she knew—some of the kids from *School of Rock*, her costars from her TV movie, and even some YouTube friends. Everyone was having a blast—most of all Lila, who held JoJo's hand as they walked down the orange carpet, beaming for every photo.

Then it was time for JoJo's big performance. Nickelodeon had asked her to perform some of her newer songs—"Every Girl's a Supergirl," "High Top Shoes," and "Only Getting Better"—along with some of her hits like "Boomerang" and "Kid in a Candy Store." JoJo squeezed Lila's hand and gave her parents a smile just before walking on stage to thunderous applause. JoJo had butterflies—the kind that came right before she did the thing she loved the most in the world. She could hardly see the crowd through the bright lights that were trained on the stage. But she knew the thousands of people in the audience were smiling and ready for her biggest, best performance yet. The lights dimmed, the crowd quieted . . . and then a spotlight switched on, illuminating JoJo and making the crowd go wild.

"Maybe you noticed something about us . . ." JoJo began. "The things we do so well, we do it better when we're together, and everyone can tell." JoJo let everything go, fueled by the crowd's cheers. As she threw herself into the song and the choreography that had become second nature, she let herself think back to the afternoon that had brought them all together. The fund-raiser had been a success in the end because it was a team effort. Even Louis's trick with the blue shampoo had been a hit. She realized she believed more in her lyrics now than she ever had before.

"Every girl's a supergirl!" JoJo finished, throwing her arms into the air. The lights dimmed, and she could finally see her audience through the spotlights. Everyone was on their feet. Then they were chanting JoJo's name. This feeling—making people happy, doing what she did best—it was what JoJo loved more than anything.

When she returned to her seat, she high-fived Lila and Mandi. "I am *so* glad you guys could come," JoJo said. "It wouldn't have been the same without you!"

"JoJo! Don't sit down yet," her dad told her, his voice thick with pride. "They're about to announce the winner in your category!" Just as he was saying it, JoJo heard her name blaring loud over the sound system.

"Looks like she's a little distracted," said the presenter, laughing, and JoJo saw her own shocked face on the JumboTron hovering high above the amphitheater. "I repeat: Our winner is . . . JoJo Siwa!"

"Ahhhh!" All of JoJo's friends leapt out of their chairs, cheering and hugging JoJo. JoJo couldn't believe it. She ran back to the stage, high-fiving everyone she passed, and accepted the orange blimp the presenter offered her. This one, she thought to herself with a smile, was undoubtedly *not* an éclair. As she cradled her trophy in one arm and waved at the crowd with the other, she realized she had everything she'd ever wanted.

"Get ready . . . to . . . get . . . slimed!" the presenter shouted, playing to the crowd.

Maybe it really was the best day ever. *Or maybe,* thought JoJo, waiting for the green gunk to fall from above, *this is only the beginning!*

# MORE BOOKS AVAILABLE BY JOJO SIWA!